THE
THREE
BILLY GOATS
GRUFF

For Kay

Paul Galdone

Clarion Books
New York

Clarion Books
a Houghton Mifflin Company imprint
215 Park Avenue South, New York, NY 10003
Copyright © 1973 by Paul Galdone
All rights reserved.
For information about permission to reproduce
selections from this book, write to Permissions,
Houghton Mifflin Company, 215 Park Avenue South, New York, NY 10003.
Library of Congress Card Number: 72-85338
ISBN: 0-395-28812-6   Paperback ISBN: 0-89919-035-9
(Previously published by The Seabury Press under ISBN: 0-8164-3080-2)
Book designed by Paul Galdone
Printed in the United States of America

HOR 40 39 38 37 36 35 34 33

THE THREE BILLY GOATS GRUFF

Once upon a time there were three Billy Goats.
They lived in a valley and the name
of all three Billy Goats was "Gruff."

There was very little grass in the valley
and the Billy Goats were hungry.
They wanted to go up the hillside
to a fine meadow full of grass and daisies
where they could eat and eat and eat, and get fat.

But on the way up there was
a bridge over a rushing river.
And under the bridge lived a Troll
who was as mean as he was ugly.

First the youngest Billy Goat Gruff
decided to cross the bridge.

"TRIP, TRAP, TRIP, TRAP!" went the bridge.

"WHO'S THAT TRIPPING OVER MY BRIDGE?"
roared the Troll.

"Oh, it's only I, the tiniest Billy Goat Gruff,"
said the Billy Goat in his very small voice.
"And I'm going to the meadow to make myself fat."

"No you're not," said the Troll,
"for I'm coming to gobble you up!"

"Oh, please don't take me. I'm too little, that I am,"
said the Billy Goat. "Wait till the second
Billy Goat Gruff comes. He's much bigger."

"Well then, be off with you," said the Troll.

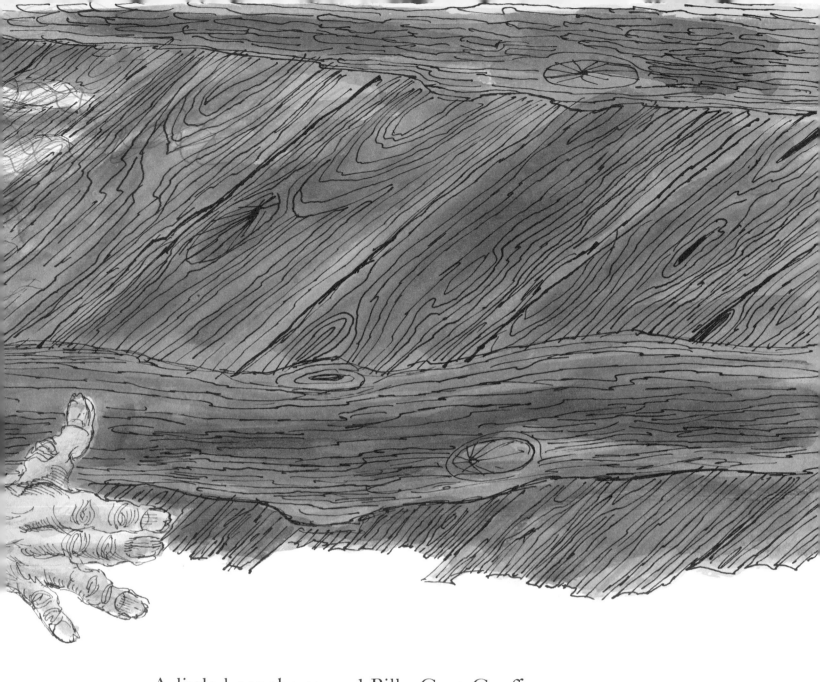

A little later the second Billy Goat Gruff came
to cross the bridge.

"TRIP, TRAP! TRIP, TRAP! TRIP, TRAP!"
went the bridge.

"WHO'S THAT TRIPPING OVER MY BRIDGE?"
roared the Troll.

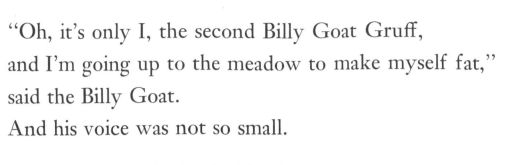

"Oh, it's only I, the second Billy Goat Gruff,
and I'm going up to the meadow to make myself fat,"
said the Billy Goat.
And his voice was not so small.

"No you're not," said the Troll,
"for I'm coming to gobble you up!"

"Oh, please don't take me. Wait a little, till the
third Billy Goat Gruff comes. He's much bigger."

"Very well, be off with you," said the Troll.

Then up came the third Billy Goat Gruff.

"TRIP, TRAP! TRIP, TRAP!
TRIP, TRAP! TRIP, TRAP!"
went the bridge.

The third Billy Goat Gruff was so heavy
that the bridge creaked and groaned under him.

"WHO'S THAT TRAMPING OVER MY BRIDGE?"
roared the Troll.

"IT IS I, THE BIG BILLY GOAT GRUFF,"
said the Billy Goat.
And his voice was as loud as the Troll's.

"Now I'm coming to gobble you up!" roared the Troll.

"Well, come along!" said the big Billy Goat Gruff.
"I've got two horns and four hard hooves.
See what you can do!"

So up climbed that mean, ugly Troll,
and the big Billy Goat Gruff butted him with his horns,
and he trampled him with his hard hooves,

and he tossed him over the bridge
into the rushing river.

Then the big Billy Goat Gruff went up the hillside to join his brothers.

In the meadow
the three Billy Goats Gruff
got so fat that they could hardly
walk home again.
They are probably there yet.

So snip, snap, snout,
This tale's told out.